Dear Black Girl

By Kaylonni Isis Turner

Copyright © 2021 by Kaylonni Isis Turner.

All rights reserved. No part of this book may be reproduced or used in any manner without written permission of the copyright owners except for the use of quotations in a book review or for educational purposes.

ISBN: 978-1-7373993-0-8

Publisher: Isis Publishing, LLC.

Dedicated to my intelligent, beautiful, hilarious, and adventurous Daughters, Nora Kay and Yara Klaire.

And to all of our Daughters: may you always know that your hair is pure magic, your skin is pure gold and your mind holds the key to the future.

Do you know that you are special and so very loved?

Do you know that you can do anything beyond the stars and above?

Do you know that your skin has been kissed by the sun, and your beautiful shade of brown makes you second to none?

Do you know that your smile gives the joy we all need to seek?

Do you know that you're brave, as brave as can be?

Do you know that you're a treasure like an oyster with a pearl?

Do you know that you are proud, proud to be who you are?

Do you know that you matter from your afro puffs to your feet?

Do you know that you are perfect just the way you are?

Kaylonni Isis Turner is the Founder, CEO, and Author of Yara Klaire Book Series, LLC.

Her passion for reading and writing budded at the early age of seven as she would sit at the dining room table, drawing and writing stories about everywhere her vivid imagination would take her. Her natural love of writing led her to earn her Bachelor's Degree in Journalism from Michigan State University.

As a Wife and Mother of three adventurous toddlers who share her infatuation with reading, Kaylonni became inspired to write children's books when she saw the need for books that revolve around characters who her children could see themselves in.

Passionate about representation and inspired by her children, Kaylonni created Yara Klaire Book Series to uplift and inspire young, Black Children through positive affirmations, beautiful imagery, and exciting adventures with characters who look just like them.

To contact Kaylonni visit:
www.YaraKlaireBooks.com
Email: Contact@YaraKlaireBooks.com
Instagram: @YaraKlaireBooks